Gossie&Gertie

Olivier Dunrea

HOUGHTON MIFFLIN HARCOURT
Boston   New York

WWW.HMHBOOKS.COM/FREEDOWNLOADS
ACCESS CODE: FRIENDS

AGES	GRADES	GUIDED READING LEVEL	READING RECOVERY LEVEL	LEXILE® LEVEL
4–6	1	E	7–8	10L

The text of this book is set in Shannon.
The illustrations are ink and watercolor on paper.

The Library of Congress Cataloging-in-Publication Data is on file.

ISBN: 978-0-618-17676-2 hardcover
IBSN: 978-0-618-74793-1 board book
ISBN: 978-0-544-10535-5 paperback reader
ISBN: 978-0-544-11443-2 paper over board reader

Manufactured in China
SCP 10 9 8 7 6 5 4 3 2 1
4500439428

For Pupper

This is Gossie.

This is Gertie.

Gossie wears bright red boots.
Gertie wears bright blue boots.

They are friends.
Best friends.

They splash in the rain.

They play hide-and-seek
in the daisies.

They dive in the pond.

They watch in the night.

They play in the haystacks.

Gossie and Gertie are
best friends.

Everywhere Gossie goes,

Gertie goes too.

"Follow me!" cried Gossie.
Gossie marched to the barn.

Gertie followed.

"Follow me!" cried Gossie.
Gossie sneaked to the sheep.

Gertie followed.

"Follow me!"
cried Gossie.

Gossie jumped
into a mud puddle.
Gertie did not follow.

"Follow me!"
shouted Gossie.

Gertie followed a
hopping frog.

"Follow me!"
shouted Gossie.

But Gertie followed
a butterfly.

"Follow me!"
shouted Gossie.

But Gertie followed
a shiny blue beetle.

"Follow me!" shouted Gossie
as she followed Gertie.

Gertie followed a trail
of grain.

"Follow me!" said Gertie.
"It's dinnertime."

Gossie followed.

Gossie and Gertie are friends.
Best friends.